Luna's Red Hat

Luna's Red Hat

An Illustrated Storybook
to Help Children Cope
with Loss and Suicide

With a **contribution by**
Dr Riet Fiddelaers-Jaspers

Emmi Smid

Jessica Kingsley *Publishers*
London and Philadelphia

Created with the professional advice of bereavement institution Werkgroep Verder,
www.werkgroepverder.be, and bereavement specialist
Dr Riet Fiddelaers-Jaspers, www.rietfiddelaers.nl

First published in 2015
by Jessica Kingsley Publishers
73 Collier Street
London N1 9BE, UK
and
400 Market Street, Suite 400
Philadelphia, PA 19106, USA

www.jkp.com

Library of Congress Cataloging in Publication Data
A CIP catalog record for this book is available from the Library of Congress

British Library Cataloguing in Publication Data
A CIP catalogue record for this book is available from the British Library

ISBN 978 1 84905 629 8
eISBN 978 1 78450 111 2

Printed and bound in China

For
Merel
and
Silke

Emmi Smid
illustration

It was the beginning of spring.
Luna was in the park and she was wearing
her mum's red summer hat.
It was a gorgeous day.

And yet, Luna felt anything but sunny.
It was exactly a year ago that it happened.

Today was not the day for feeling sunny.

Dad arrived with a picnic basket.
"I thought you would be here," he said.
"That hat suits you," he smiled,
"you look just like Mum."

Luna took off the hat and threw it aside.
"I don't look like Mum!" she said.
"You've got her frown!" Dad grinned.

Luna got up, kicked the hat
and shouted:

"I am nothing like Mum!"

Dad reached for Luna's hand and said:
"Now what's with the frown, Luna-Clown?"
Luna usually liked it when Dad called her Luna-Clown,
but not today.

Today was not the day for liking things.

"I am not like Mum!" said Luna.

"Because I wouldn't just stop living when I wanted to!
People you love don't get to stop living and leave you behind!"

"I see," said Dad.
"And you are not like Mum either, right?" said Luna.
"No," said Dad, "that hat would make me look silly."
Luna tried to suppress a smile.

Today was not the day for smiling.

"Stop being silly!
I mean that you are not going to leave me, right?" said Luna.

"No, I'm not going to leave you, Luna Love.
We are going to have a picnic!" said Dad.

"Come sit, Luna," said Dad. "You are right.
Normally Mums don't stop living when they want to,
and you have every right to be angry."

"Mum didn't want to leave us,
and she didn't want to die, but she just couldn't
find another way out," said Dad.

"Why not?" asked Luna.
"Mum was very ill. She didn't look ill,
 but that was because the illness was hiding inside her head,"
 said Dad.
"What was it doing there?" said Luna.
"The illness made Mum feel very unhappy,
 for a really long time," said Dad.

"But why didn't the doctors make her feel better?" asked Luna. "Because they couldn't. Unfortunately sometimes even doctors don't have all the answers," said Dad.

"What if I had been less naughty?" said Luna.

"My Lulu," said Dad,
"some days you were Loopy-Luna,
some days you were Lulu-Loud...

...and Mum loved every
day she spent with her
lovely Luna!"

"So it wasn't my fault?" said Luna.
"No," said Dad. "It wasn't your fault, it wasn't my fault,
and it wasn't Mum's fault either."

"Daffodils," said Luna. "Mum's favourite flowers.
Remember how she used to fill the house with daffodils?"
"Yes," said Dad.

"Let's pick some and take them to Mum," said Luna.

"I miss Mum,"
said Luna.

"I know,"
said Dad,
"I miss Mum too."

Dad picked up the hat.
"Do you remember that day when we had a picnic in the park, and Mum was wearing this hat?" said Dad.
"Yes," said Luna.

"The wind threw Mum's hat in the pond,
and you jumped in the water to save it!
And then Mum gave you a cupcake for being her
Hat Hero!" Luna giggled.

"Maybe I'll wear Mum's hat after all," said Luna.

"I think the hat should be yours," said Dad.

"Ok then," said Luna.

"Do you want a cupcake?"
said Luna.

"Yes please!"
said Dad.

Guide for Parents
By Bereavement Specialist Dr Riet Fiddelaers-Jaspers

Suicide always evokes a shock, not just for the family, but also for everyone around them. Children will have to deal with those reactions. It's not easy to explain to children that someone has ended their life. You might want to hold back from telling your child the truth, in order to protect them. This is understandable, yet it is necessary to be honest. Children have the right to know. By telling them what has happened in a careful yet clear manner, children can learn to understand the situation, and will feel that they are taken seriously.

How children understand death

Very young children are not capable of understanding death, yet they will be very aware that something serious is going on. Even babies will pick up on the tension and emotions around them, which might unsettle them. You can explain to babies and toddlers why you feel sad. They might not fully comprehend, but they will understand to a certain level. It is important that they feel that they are a part of the situation. Your presence will calm them down and they will feel consoled.

Between the ages of three and six children will be able to understand your words, but will not necessarily understand that death is something final. You will have to explain clearly that once someone has died they will not come back to life.

From six to nine years old children will start to realise that death is a final thing, yet they will have difficulties comprehending it. The concept is confusing and may cause anxiety. It is not unusual for six- to nine-year-olds to return to comforting habits, such as sucking their thumb. They might become clingy or show signs of fear of abandonment.

You may find that your child asks you practical and factual questions. Young children may take words quite literally, so it is important to use clear, simple sentences. In order to comprehend the situation, children between the ages of nine and twelve might ask you lots of questions, some of which you do not even want to think about yourself.

How to inform your child

How do you tell your child that the person who died has committed suicide? Children intuitively know when something is the matter. When you are honest, it will help them to calm down and it will make them feel included, rather than feeling left alone with their emotions and questions. Besides that, there is a chance that they might find out that it was suicide via neighbours or friends at school. It is important that they hear it from someone they trust, such as a parent. You can, potentially with the advice and support of others, choose your words carefully to inform your child. This way you will maintain the trust between the two of you. If the child finds out through someone else, they might wonder why "everyone" apart from them knows about it. Your child has the right to know what happened, as it will have a positive influence on their grief.

Start with an introductory sentence to get the child's attention: "I'm finding it very hard to have to tell you this. . .", then tell them the message, as straight and clear as possible: "Dad has killed himself."

Questions from children

In the following days and months children will have a lot of questions for you: "Why did he do it?" "How did she do it?" "Did no one notice something was wrong with him?" "Why did she not tell me?" "Couldn't he have stayed for me?"

Allow children to ask questions, even when they are hard for you to answer. Be honest if you do not have an answer; do not make any answers up. Try to answer their practical questions too, but be careful about going into too much detail.

Make sure to look after yourself as well, and create a network of support around you. This will show your child that they do not need to look after you, and that they are allowed to focus on their own grief.

Dr Riet Fiddelaers-Jaspers is a well-known bereavement specialist in the Netherlands. She has written numerous books about bereavement and suicide, for children as well as parents.
www.rietfiddelaers.nl

For more information about coping after a suicide visit www.nhs.uk